To Olivia and Tenzin
—A.W.

To my special friends Mati and Lola
—S.V.

Alice Walker

...

There Is a Flower at the Tip of My Nose Smelling Me

Illustrations by

Stefano Vitale

HarperCollins Publishers

There is a flower
At the tip
Of my nose
Smelling
Me.

There is a sky
At the end
Of my
Eye
Seeing
Me.

There is a road
At the bottom
Of my
Foot
Walking me.

There is a dog
At the end
Of my leash
Holding
Me.

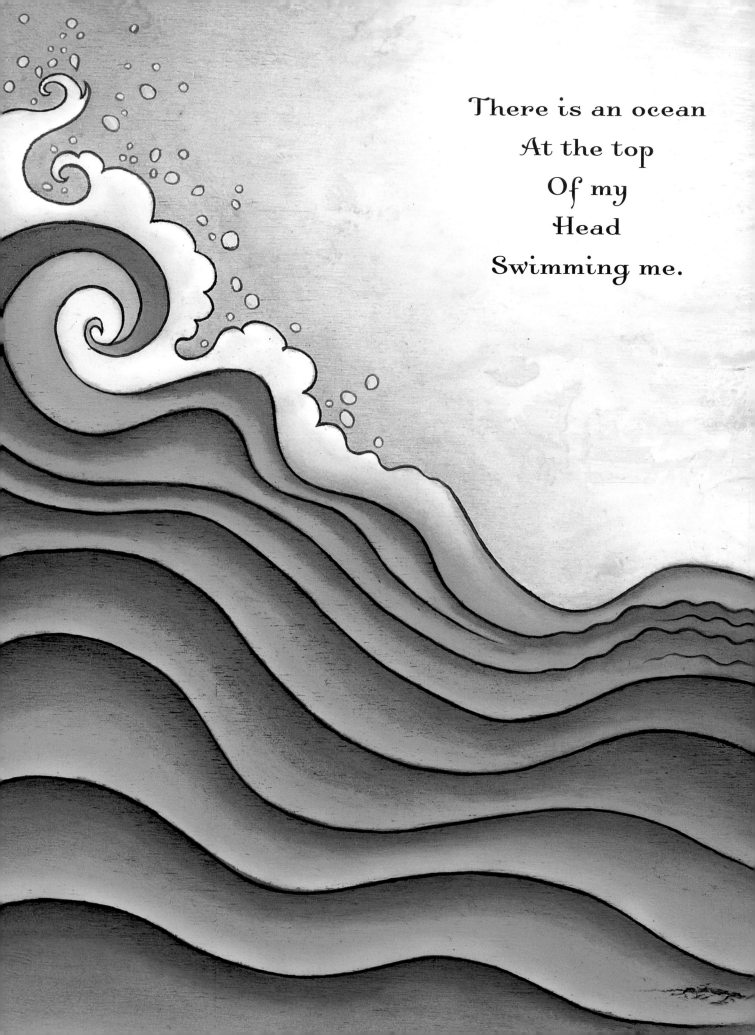

There is an ocean
At the top
Of my
Head
Swimming me.

There is a sunrise

At the edge

Of

My skin

Praising

Me.

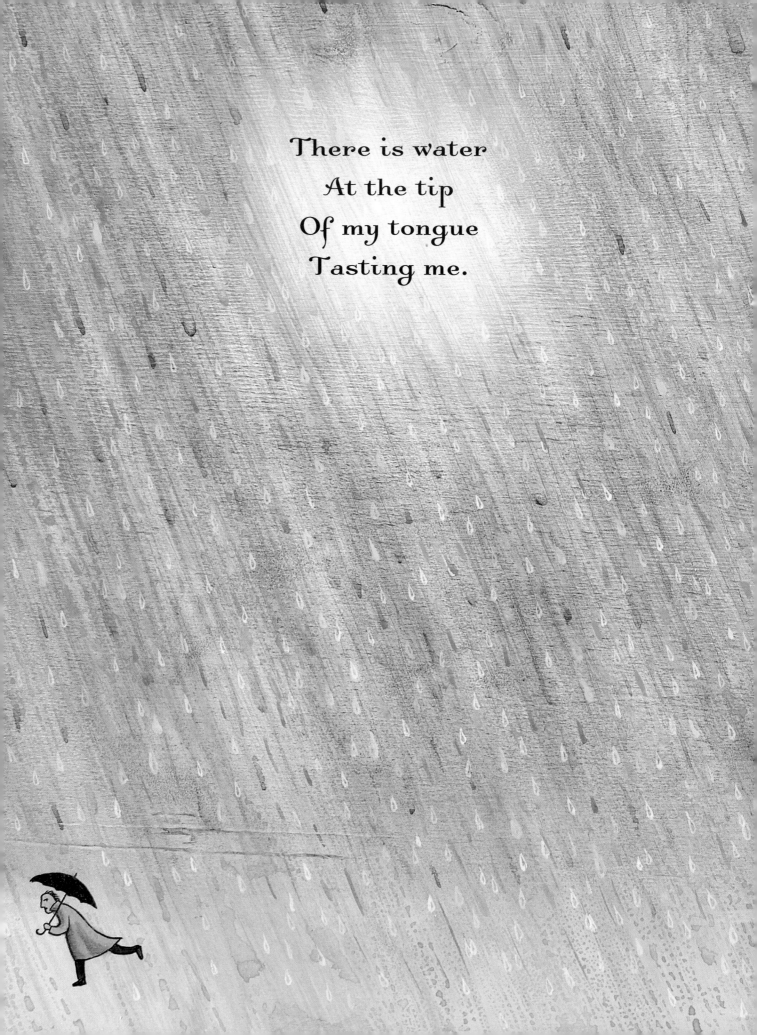

There is water
At the tip
Of my tongue
Tasting me.

There is a song
Deep in
My body
Singing
Me.

There is a dance
That lives
In my bones
Dancing
Me.

There is a poem
In the cradle
Of my Soul
Rocking me.

There is a pen
Nestled
In my hand
Writing
Me.

There is a story
At the end
Of my arms
Telling
Me!

A Note from the Author

One day I went walking in the forest near my house with my dog, along an old logging trail. Redwoods rose to left and right, the sky was brilliant blue with a few threads of clouds, the earth was scented with spring. As I walked, the wonder of myself as part of all this overcame me. I began to sing: "I come out of You, my Love. I come out of You!" Over and over, with the greatest gratitude and joy. As soon as I got home, my big black lab trotting just as happily beside me, I wrote this book, which was not a book then, but a thank you note.

• • •

There Is a Flower at the Tip of My Nose Smelling Me
Text copyright © 2006 by Alice Walker
Illustrations copyright © 2006 by Stefano Vitale
Manufactured in China.
All rights reserved.
www.harperchildrens.com

Library of Congress Cataloging-in-Publication Data
Walker, Alice, date.
    There is a flower at the tip of my nose smelling me / by Alice Walker;
illustrated by Stefano Vitale. — 1st ed.
        p.   cm.
    ISBN-10: 0-06-057080-6 (trade bdg.) — ISBN-13: 978-0-06-057080-4 (trade bdg.)
    ISBN-10: 0-06-057081-4 (lib. bdg.) — ISBN-13: 978-0-06-057081-1 (lib. bdg.)
    1. Self—Juvenile poetry. 2. Children's poetry, American. I. Vitale, Stefano.
II. Title.
PS3573.A425T467 2006
811'.54—dc22   2005001627

Design by Martha Rago
1 2 3 4 5 6 7 8 9 10 ❖ First Edition